Trouble at
Camp Treehouse

"You know who I think could have stolen Lauren's camera?" Bess said to Nancy. "That creep David Mulholland."

Just then David came over to the Arts and Crafts table and stood right near Nancy, Bess, and Lauren. He had a shoe box in one hand.

"What's in the shoe box?" Mike Silver asked.

David's eyes twinkled. "Oh, nothing. Just something I'll bet you *girls* would love to have—a gold ring."

"Where did you get a gold ring?" Nancy asked suspiciously.

"Yeah, that's what I'd like to know," Lauren said. Under her breath she whispered to Nancy, "I'll bet he stole that, too!"

The Nancy Drew Notebooks

THE
NANCY DREW
NOTEBOOKS®

#7

Trouble at Camp Treehouse

CAROLYN KEENE
ILLUSTRATED BY ANTHONY ACCARDO

Winnona Park
Elementary School

Aladdin Paperbacks
New York   London   Toronto   Sydney   Singapore

This book is a work of fiction. Any references to historical events, real people, or real locales are used fictitiously. Other names, characters, places, and incidents are the product of the author's imagination, and any resemblance to actual events or locales or persons, living or dead, is entirely coincidental.

First Aladdin Paperbacks edition January 2002
First Minstrel Books edition July 1995

Copyright © 1995 by Simon & Schuster, Inc.
Produced by Mega-Books, Inc.

ALADDIN PAPERBACKS
An imprint of Simon & Schuster
Children's Publishing Division
1230 Avenue of the Americas
New York, NY 10020

The text of this book was set in Excelsior.

Printed in the United States of America
10 9

NANCY DREW and THE NANCY DREW NOTEBOOKS
are registered trademarks of Simon & Schuster, Inc.

ISBN 0-671-87951-0

1

Worms for Bess

No, no, no," Bess Marvin said to her best friend, Nancy Drew. She shook her head hard. Her blond hair swung back and forth across her shoulders. "I'll do anything but that. Anything! I'd rather eat worms!"

Eight-year-old Nancy laughed. "That's not true," she said. "You wouldn't even *touch* a worm!"

"Okay, you're right," Bess said. "I wouldn't eat a worm. But if I had to, I'd rather eat worms than go swimming."

Nancy sighed and flopped down on her bunk bed. She lay across the mattress, with her legs hanging off one side. She stared at the cabin floor.

I want to go swimming, Nancy thought. But I don't want to fight with my best friend.

Nancy and Bess had been going to day camp together all summer. Now it was August. As a special treat, all the day campers were spending a long weekend at a sleep-away camp called Camp Treehouse.

The campers had arrived the afternoon before. There had been a special picnic dinner to welcome them. Now it was Saturday morning. Nancy was excited about everything—and especially about swimming. The lake was clear and blue. But Bess didn't want to swim. She was afraid of the water.

"You can come swimming with me," a tall girl across the cabin said to Nancy.

Nancy looked up and saw Lauren

Soules smiling at her. Lauren was a new friend Nancy had made at day camp. She had friendly brown eyes and long, dark brown hair. Nancy liked her because Lauren was never mean to anyone.

"Yeah, come with us," Dana Smiley said. Dana was always in a hurry. Now she was hurrying to put on her bathing suit. Even before breakfast!

"Oh, please don't," Bess begged Nancy. "I thought we were going to stay together. It's more fun that way. Please? I'll do anything else. Anything."

"But why won't you even try swimming?" Nancy asked. "You like wading in the pool at home."

"That's different," Bess said. "Here they make you put your face in the water, and blow bubbles."

"How do you know?" Nancy asked.

"Nora told me," Bess said.

Nancy looked over at Nora Chang. She was sitting on her bunk by the wall with her best friend, Joanna Richter. Joanna had the bunk next to hers.

Nora and Joanna had been best friends for a long time. Nora had dark brown eyes and long black hair. Joanna had shoulder-length red hair and blue eyes, and she wore glasses.

The two girls didn't look alike. But they often dressed alike and wore their hair alike. Today they were both wearing pigtails. Their pigtails bounced up and down as they both nodded.

"It's true," Nora said. "You have to blow bubbles. That's why we're not doing it, either."

"Besides that," Bess said, "I bet creeps like David Mulholland or Mike Silver would swim up behind me and pull me under." Bess shuddered. "Ugh."

"Okay," Nancy said, finally giving in to Bess. She sat up, and her blue eyes sparkled. "How about horseback riding?"

"Oh, not horses!" Bess said. "What if I fall?"

"Bess Marvin, you're chicken about everything!" Nancy said, laughing. She tossed a pillow at Bess, who was in the bunk across from Nancy's.

Bess ducked and laughed, too. "Yeah, I guess I am," she said. She pulled a headband over her head, then pushed it up over her hair. "Okay," Bess agreed. "Maybe I'll try horseback riding. But only if they have a really small horse."

"Great," Nancy said, sitting up.

"Girls, are you all dressed for breakfast?" a voice called.

Nancy turned to look over her shoulder. Mary Ann Remar was coming in through the cabin's screen door. She had been one of the counselors at day camp. Now she was the counselor in the Bluebird cabin. She was short and athletic, with chin-length brown hair.

Nancy bounced off the bed and hurried to put on her sneakers. Her stomach rumbled. She was hungry.

"Come on, Bluebirds," Mary Ann said.

All the girls gathered near the screen door. All except one. Lauren was still looking for something in her duffel bag.

"Now, before we go," Mary Ann said, "I want to review the camp rules one more time. First, no one is allowed to go anywhere alone. Not unless you have special permission from a counselor. Otherwise, you must always have a buddy."

Then Mary Ann told them everything else they needed to know. Where to sit in the dining hall. How to sign up for morning activities and afternoon activities. What to do when a loud bell rang three times.

"That's the signal for everyone to go to the next activity," Mary Ann explained.

I wish someone would ring a bell right now, Nancy thought—a breakfast bell. I'm ready to go to the eating activity.

"What if you don't know what activity you want to sign up for?" Bess asked, sounding worried.

"Well, you can talk to me about that at breakfast," Mary Ann said. "I'm sure we can find something you'll like. How about the treehouse?"

"What's that?" Dana asked quickly.

"Didn't you see it?" Nora said. Her brown eyes shone with excitement. "It's a huge treehouse in an oak tree over by the Arts and Crafts shop."

"Yeah. It's gigantic," Joanna agreed. "It has ramps and towers and ladders and special rooms—and everything."

"That's how Camp Treehouse got its name," Mary Ann explained.

"Oh," Dana said, her green eyes lighting up. "It sounds like fun. Now I don't know whether to pick swimming or treehouse."

"They're both fun," Mary Ann said. "But treehouse is very popular. Only fifteen kids can play there at one time. Maybe you should wait and sign up for that in the afternoon."

"Well, what are we waiting for? Let's go," Dana said eagerly.

"Lauren, are you ready?" Mary Ann called.

Nancy looked over at Lauren, who was sitting on her bed staring at the floor. Her face was red, and she looked as if she was going to cry. Her dark brown eyes were filled with tears.

"Lauren? What's wrong?" Mary Ann asked.

Lauren raised her eyes. "My camera has been stolen!" she cried.

2

Camera Thief

"Stolen!" Mary Ann Remar said. She hurried over to Lauren and put her arm around the girl.

"How awful!" Dana blurted out. "Someone in here must have stolen it."

"No way," Mary Ann said, glancing up at the Bluebird campers. "No one in here would steal your camera, Lauren."

Right, Nancy thought. They wouldn't. Would they?

Nancy sneaked a look at the other girls, who were still huddled near the door. Besides Nancy, there were Bess, Dana, Nora, and Joanna.

Nora and Joanna looked very serious and quiet. They moved off to one side and whispered. Then they kept glancing over at everyone else with wide, worried eyes.

"Well, it's missing," Lauren said, her voice cracking. "Look."

She reached for her duffel bag on the floor and opened it wide. Everyone moved in to get a closer look.

As Mary Ann searched in the duffel, Nancy eyed the contents, too. She saw a neatly rolled-up sweatshirt. Rolled-up jeans. A row of rolled-up socks. Folded pink shorts. A bathing suit. A plastic bag with soap and toothbrush.

Everything but a camera.

A big tear spilled out of Lauren's eye and rolled down one cheek.

"Maybe you didn't bring it with you to camp," Mary Ann said, trying to comfort her.

"But I did," Lauren said in a squeaky

voice. "I saw it. It was sitting on my bed when my mom packed my clothes."

"Well, then maybe you lost it somewhere," Mary Ann said. "Remember how you've been losing things all summer? You lost your headband one week at day camp. And you lost your snack money another time."

"That's not fair," Lauren cried. "That's what my mom will think. But I promised her . . . I promised her . . ."

Lauren was so upset, she choked on the words. Then big tears overflowed from both eyes and rolled down her cheeks. Nancy felt really sorry for her.

"It's okay," Mary Ann said, hugging Lauren tightly with one arm around her shoulder. "Your camera will probably turn up somewhere. Don't worry. You can look for it later."

Nancy rushed over to Lauren and took her hand. "Come on," Nancy said. "Let's go have breakfast. Then you can tell me what happened. I'll help you find your camera."

"Nancy is great at finding things," Bess said.

"Really?" Lauren said.

"Yes, definitely," Bess said.

Lauren wiped away her tears and stood up. "Great!" she said. "Thanks, Nancy."

Before they left the cabin, Nancy hurried to her own duffel bag. She checked to make sure her special blue notebook—the one with the pocket inside—was still there. Nancy always used it to take notes when she was trying to solve a mystery.

On the way to the dining hall, Lauren talked to Nancy about the camera.

"It's a really good camera. I had to beg my parents to buy it," Lauren said. "They didn't want to, because they thought I would lose it. I lose things a lot. But I promised my mom I would take extra good care of it. That's why I have to find it—or else she'll never trust me again."

Nancy nodded to show she was listening. But as they walked to the dining hall, she looked around her. She remembered many things about the camp from the afternoon before. Other things were new. Nancy was trying to learn her way around and make a map of the camp in her mind.

The five cabins for girls were all in the woods, up a small hill. At the bottom of the hill were three activity areas. One was Arts and Crafts. One was Music. And one was the treehouse.

Then they came to the middle of the camp, to a big clearing. That was where the campfires were held. From the clearing, a trail led down to the lake.

Finally Nancy and her cabin mates reached the dining hall on the other side of camp. The boys' cabins and the horse stables were nearby.

All the girls in Nancy's cabin rushed up the steps into the large building.

"I love it here," Nancy said.

"Yeah," Bess said. She added, "Too bad they let the boys come."

Nancy, Bess, and Lauren all giggled.

Inside, Nancy looked around. There were lots of wooden tables and chairs. Kids from all the cabins were hurrying to sit down. Colorful banners hung from the ceiling.

Mary Ann Remar led the girls to a round table in the corner near a screened window. "This is where the Bluebirds will sit for all meals," she told them.

"I'm going to sit near Joanna and Nora," Nancy whispered to Bess and Lauren. "I want to ask them some questions."

"Okay," Bess said. "I'll sit with Dana and do the same thing."

Nancy waited for Nora and Joanna to find seats. They always did everything together. Then Nancy sat down next to Joanna.

Soon platters of blueberry pancakes were served. Nancy took three pancakes and poured syrup on them.

"Joanna," Nancy said, cutting into her pancakes. "Did you see anyone come into our cabin yesterday? After we got to camp?"

"Nope," Joanna said. She was eating pancakes, too. "We were all in there together before dinner, remember? But someone could have sneaked in and stolen Lauren's camera while we were having our picnic dinner, don't you think?"

"Maybe," Nancy said.

But she didn't really think so. How could anyone get away? All the campers had to stay together with their counselors, especially on the first night.

"Then we came back from the picnic," Nora said, joining in. "Dana and Joanna and I played cards, and then it was time to get ready for bed. Joanna and I went to the bathroom to brush our teeth. Maybe someone stole the camera then."

"Hmmm," Nancy said. She thought about that. The bathrooms were in a small building across from the cabin. "What time was that?"

"I don't know," Joanna said. She pushed her glasses into place on her nose. "But we were gone for about fifteen minutes."

Nancy took out her notebook. She wrote down: "Nora and Joanna in bathroom for fifteen minutes after dinner."

"What are you writing?" Nora asked, trying to peek at Nancy's notebook.

17

"Just some notes," Nancy said. Then she pushed back her chair. "Excuse me," Nancy said. "I want to sit with Bess for a minute."

She picked up her plate and walked around the table. She tapped Lauren on the shoulder. "Do you mind if I trade places with you?" Nancy said.

Lauren looked up from her breakfast, surprised. "Okay," she said.

She got up and traded seats with Nancy.

For a while Nancy ate her breakfast and listened while Bess talked to Dana. Dana talked very fast. Sometimes she talked with her mouth full. But she said she didn't know anything about Lauren's camera.

Then Nancy tapped Bess's arm and pulled her to one side.

"What's up?" Bess asked.

"Lots," Nancy said, whispering. "I think I have a suspect."

"Who?" Bess asked.

Nancy put her mouth right next to Bess's ear. She lowered her voice so that it was even quieter than a whisper.

"You're sitting right next to her," Nancy said. "It's Dana."

3

Arts and Creeps

Bess's blue eyes opened wide. "Dana is the suspect?" she whispered back. "But why?"

"I'll have to tell you later," Nancy said, glancing around.

Everyone else at the table was talking and laughing as they finished breakfast—even Dana. She was telling a joke to someone across the table. But Nancy didn't want to take any chances. She didn't want anyone—and especially Dana—to overhear.

"What are you going to do?" Bess whispered to Nancy.

"I'm going to follow her today," Nancy said very softly. "To see if she acts guilty. Or steals something else. Or tells someone she took Lauren's camera."

"Follow her?" Bess whispered. "But she's going swimming."

Before Nancy could answer, one of the counselors at the far end of the room got up to speak. "It's time to sign up for morning activities," the counselor said. "The sign-up table is outside the dining hall."

"Let's go!" Dana said, jumping up. "I want to go swimming!"

"Sit down," Mary Ann said. "We'll go when it's our turn. Right now, it's the Eagles' turn."

"No fair! They'll get all the good stuff," Dana complained.

"Maybe," Mary Ann said. "But then maybe we'll get to go first this afternoon."

"Oh, *please* don't sign up for swimming," Bess begged Nancy quietly. "Please. I don't want to be left all alone."

Nancy bit her lip. She didn't want to leave Bess alone. But she didn't want to leave the mystery without solving it, either.

"Okay," Nancy finally said. "I'll do what you want this morning. But this afternoon I'm going to follow Dana."

Soon it was the Bluebirds' turn to sign up. All the girls jumped up and ran to the sign-up table. Nancy and Bess chose Arts and Crafts. Lauren did, too. She said she wanted to stay with Nancy. Then all three girls followed Mary Ann to Arts and Crafts. The other campers went with the other counselors to the activities for which they had signed up.

On the way, Nancy told Lauren and Bess about her suspect. "Why do you think it's Dana?" Lauren asked.

"Because I remember what happened

yesterday when we got here," Nancy said. "We all stayed together until after dinner. Then Mary Ann called us outside to see the raccoon."

"Right," Lauren said, remembering. "But Dana, Nora, and Joanna didn't want to come. They were playing cards."

"Right," Nancy said.

"So that means any one of them could have taken it," Bess said.

"Not really," Nancy said. "Would you steal a camera when someone else was watching?"

"I guess not," Bess said.

"Anyway, Nora told me that she and Joanna went to the bathroom for about fifteen minutes to brush their teeth," Nancy went on. "They left Dana in the cabin, alone. She could have taken the camera then."

Lauren was quiet for a moment. She

looked sad. "Why would Dana do something so mean?" she asked.

"We don't know for sure that she even did it," Nancy said as they took their seats in the Arts and Crafts room.

For the next ten minutes, Nancy and her friends couldn't talk. They had to listen to Linda, the Arts and Crafts counselor. Linda had super-frizzy long blond hair. Nancy liked the way Linda tied her hair up with six different colored ribbons.

Linda explained how to use the paints and brushes without making a big mess. Finally the paper, brushes, and paper cups full of poster paint were passed out.

"Let's take these things outside," Linda said. "We can do our art projects on the picnic tables near the treehouse. It's too nice a day to stay inside."

"Excuse me," Lauren called out,

raising her hand. "May I have a paper towel?"

"Sure, but what for?" Linda said.

Lauren unbuckled her watch and held it up. "I want to wrap up my watch, so I won't get it messy with paint."

"Oh, good idea," Linda said as she handed a paper towel to Lauren.

Pretty soon all the girls in the room were rolling their watches and bracelets up in paper towels.

Some of the boys in the room laughed. "What a dumb idea," Mike Silver said.

"Ignore him," Bess said to Lauren. "He's a jerk."

Then all the kids picked up their art supplies and went outside.

"You know who *I* think could have stolen Lauren's camera?" Bess said as she climbed onto the picnic table bench.

"Who?" Nancy asked.

"That creep David Mulholland."

Hmm, Nancy thought. David Mulholland. He had been playing pranks on the girls all summer at day camp. One time he had crawled under a picnic table and tied Nancy's shoelaces together.

And on the bus, on the way to sleep-away camp, he put a bug in Nora's hair.

"Could be," Nancy said. "Almost anyone could have sneaked away from dinner and gone into our cabin."

"Or taken it in the night," Lauren said. "Like a cat burglar!"

"Oooh, do you think so?" Bess said.

Nancy shrugged. Would someone really sneak into their cabin at night? In the dark? And steal something from a duffel bag? She didn't think so, but she didn't know for sure.

"Hey, look!" Bess cried, pointing to the treehouse. "It's him!"

Nancy looked up quickly and saw just the top of David Mulholland's head. He was hiding behind a ramp leading up to a platform.

"Boo!" David said, jumping out from behind the ramp. He had a shoe box in one hand.

Bess made a face and turned up her nose at him. Lauren frowned, too.

"Hey, David! Come sit here!" Mike Silver called. He was sitting at the end of Nancy's table.

David came over and stood at the other end of the table, right near Nancy, Bess, and Lauren. "Okay. But I can't stay," David said.

"What's in the shoe box?" Mike asked.

"In here?" David's eyes twinkled. He put the shoe box on the table. "Oh, nothing. Just something I'll bet you *girls* would love to have."

"What?" Bess asked.

"A ring," David said. "A gold ring."

Lauren's head snapped up, and she gave Nancy a questioning look.

"Where did you get a gold ring?" Nancy asked suspiciously.

"Yeah, that's what I'd like to know," Lauren said. Under her breath she whispered to Nancy, "I'll bet he stole it."

"I found it in the sand, down by the lake," David declared. "Ha-ha. Too bad you didn't find it first. And too bad you'll never get to see it, either."

He pulled the box toward him, moving it farther away from the girls.

Then he looked up suddenly, staring at the treehouse.

"Uh-oh. Someone's taking my turn in the tower," he said. He turned around, cupped his hands to his mouth, and shouted, "Hey! Wait for me! It's my turn!"

Then he ran off, leaving the shoe box behind.

"He forgot his precious gold ring," Bess said. She stared at the box with curiosity.

"Well, let's open it!" Lauren cried with excitement.

Putting the shoe box right in front of her, she leaned forward and lifted the lid.

"Arghh! No!" she cried as something leapt out of the box and sprang toward her.

4

Hide-and-Go-Treehouse

Help!" Lauren cried as two frogs hopped out of the shoe box.

Lauren jumped up and tried to scramble backward. But she was too late. One of the frogs had already knocked over a cup of red paint. Its belly and legs were coated with paint as it hopped toward her.

"It's coming to get me!" Lauren screamed.

Instantly the frog leapt into her lap. It smeared red paint all over her clothes. "Eeee! Get me out of here!" Bess screamed as the other frog jumped toward her. Bess almost fell off the bench as she tried to stand up and get away as fast as possible.

"Yikes!" Nancy cried. She scrambled to her feet, too.

"Haa-haaa-haaa!" Mike Silver screamed. He laughed so hard that he had to bend over and hold his stomach.

"Oooh! Look at me! I could kill that David Mulholland!" Lauren said. She held out her messy hands and stared down at her paint-covered lap.

"What's wrong? What happened here?" Linda asked, hurrying over.

"David brought a box of frogs over here!" Lauren screamed. "And they hopped all over everything! Look at my clothes!"

"Okay, okay, calm down," Linda said. "You can go clean up and change your clothes. The paint is tempera. It won't hurt you, and it will wash out. Don't worry. Do you know the way back to your cabin by yourself?"

"Sure," Lauren said. "It's just up that hill."

"Okay," Linda said. "Go on. But come right back."

"See?" Bess said, nudging Nancy and speaking softly. "I told you David Mulholland was a creep. He probably stole her camera as a joke."

Nancy thought about that for a minute. It *did* seem as if David would do anything to make girls mad.

"Let's sneak over to the treehouse to see what he's doing," Nancy said.

Bess's eyes lit up.

"Really?" Bess said. "The treehouse looks like so much fun! But won't we get in trouble?"

"Don't worry," Nancy said. Quickly Nancy scooped up the shoe box. She carried it over to Linda, who was helping some kids at another table. "This belongs to a boy in the treehouse,"

Nancy said. "Bess and I are going to take it back to him. Okay?"

"Okay," Linda said. "But don't go anywhere else."

The treehouse was only a few steps away. But Nancy didn't want David to know that she was spying on him.

She put her finger to her lips. "Shhh," she whispered to Bess. "Everyone else is playing hide-and-seek in the treehouse. So let's hide, too."

Bess giggled. "Okay. I love hide-and-seek," she said.

As quietly as they could, both girls climbed the ramp. It led up to the lowest platform in the treehouse. From there, they could walk along a whole series of bridges and ramps, leading to different rooms.

"I'm just going to leave the shoe box here," Nancy said. She put it down on the ramp.

"Now what?" Bess asked.

"Now we spy on him," Nancy said.

Pretty soon the girls were caught up in the fun. They sneaked into the tower and hid. From the tower window they watched for David.

"There he is!" Bess pointed.

Nancy looked and saw David on the lowest platform, way below.

"Let's follow him," Nancy said, hurrying out of the tower.

She ran across the rope bridge toward the huge branch of the oak tree. From the bridge, she could look down and see David.

Just then a red-haired boy came running onto the rope bridge.

"Tag—you're it!" he said, tagging Nancy on the arm.

"No, I'm not," Nancy said. "We aren't even playing. We're just visiting."

The boy cocked his head to one side.

"That's not fair," he said. "You can't just visit."

"We are," Bess insisted.

The boy looked annoyed, but he shrugged and ran across the bridge to the other side.

Nancy bent down and picked up an acorn. Then she stood near the bridge railing. She looked for David on the low platform. He was still there.

"Tag—you're it!" Nancy called, tossing the acorn down on David's head.

"Ow!" David cried, putting his hand up.

"We got him!" Bess screamed. Nancy and Bess giggled and then ran across the rope bridge to hide.

But a moment later a whistle blew.

"All in free!" a counselor called from below. "Everybody out of the tree!"

Nancy looked down and saw the treehouse counselor. He was named Frank. He blew his whistle again.

Nancy and Bess climbed down a wooden ladder to the next level. Then they walked down a ramp that led to the ground.

All the other kids from the treehouse gathered around.

"I just found a pair of glasses on the ground," Frank said. "Do these belong to anyone here?"

Nancy looked at them carefully. They were sunglasses, with a red-and-white-striped frame.

"I know whose they are," Nancy said, raising her hand.

"Whose?" Frank asked.

"Those are Mary Ann Remar's. She's our counselor in Bluebird cabin," Nancy said.

"Oh, good," Frank said. "How would you like to take them back to your cabin for me? I don't know where Mary Ann is right now, and I don't want them to get broken."

Before Nancy could answer, David Mulholland started jumping up and down.

"Let me! Let me!" he said. "I'll take them back."

"Okay," Frank said. He handed the glasses to David. "But you must come right back."

"That creep!" Bess said. "Why did he want to go to our cabin so badly?"

"I don't know," Nancy said. "But I have a guess."

"What?" Bess asked.

"Maybe he's going to try to steal something else," Nancy said. "Let's keep following him!"

5

The Trouble with David

Nancy watched as David Mulholland took Mary Ann's glasses from Frank. He had a sneaky grin on his face.

"He's up to something," Nancy whispered. "Let's find out what it is."

David headed toward the path. But before Nancy and Bess could catch up with him, he stopped. He spun around and smacked his forehead with his hands.

"Stupid me!" he said to Frank. "I forgot to ask you—where's the Blue-bird cabin?"

"Don't you know?" Frank said with

a little laugh. "It's right next to all the other girls' cabins."

"Yeah, but where *are* the other girls' cabins?" David said.

Frank laughed again. "If you don't know, then why did you offer to take the glasses back?"

David shrugged, and his face turned red. "I don't know," he said.

Nancy and Bess huddled together at the outer edge of the group.

"He was going to do something," Bess whispered. "See how guilty he looks?"

"Yes," Nancy agreed. "But he couldn't have stolen Lauren's camera. He doesn't even know where our cabin is."

Bess's shoulders slumped. "I guess not," she said. "He was probably just going to play another trick on us."

"Uh, excuse me," Frank called pointing to Nancy. "What's your name?"

"Nancy. Nancy Drew."

"Oh, good. Well, Nancy could you take these glasses up to your cabin? That's probably a better idea anyway."

"Sure," Nancy said. "May Bess come with me?"

Frank nodded. Then Nancy and Bess hurried to take the glasses from David.

"Ha-ha," Bess said, sticking her tongue out at him.

"Jerk," David said. Then he made a face and sniffed the air near Bess. "Ew, yuk. Do I smell frogs?"

"Creep!" Bess said, giving him a dirty look.

David burst out laughing and ran back to his group.

"Now what?" Bess asked Nancy.

"Now we take the glasses up to our cabin," Nancy said.

By the time Nancy and Bess got there, Lauren was just coming out. She was wearing a pair of clean pink shorts and a matching pink T-shirt. A pretty silver locket hung around her neck. Her long dark brown hair was combed, and she had a pink scrunchie in it.

Just then a bell rang three times.

"What does that mean?" Bess asked. "I forget."

"Time to go to the next activity," Nancy said.

Nancy put the sunglasses on Mary Ann's bed. Then all three girls ran down the hill and hurried across the camp to the soccer field. That's where the Bluebirds were supposed to go after their first activity.

Nancy and her cabin mates played soccer against the Sparrows' cabin. Finally the bell rang again.

"I know what that means," Bess said. "Lunch. And I'm hungry."

Nancy, Bess, and Lauren all walked together to the dining hall.

"I still want to keep an eye on Dana,"

Nancy said softly before they went to their table. "So let's sign up for whatever activity she signs up for this afternoon."

"Okay," Bess agreed. "As long as it's not swimming."

After lunch the Cardinals were called first to sign up. Then came the Goldfinches and the Chickadees. The Bluebirds were fourth.

Nancy, Bess, and Lauren hung back. They waited to see what Dana would choose.

"Phooey!" Dana said, stamping her foot. "Treehouse is full. I wanted the treehouse."

"Maybe you'll get to do it tomorrow," Mary Ann said with a sigh.

Dana frowned, but finally she picked volleyball.

"Oh, that sounds like fun," Nancy said to Bess. "Let's do volleyball."

Bess put her hand over her mouth

and giggled. "What a fake," she said under her breath.

"Don't make me laugh," Nancy said, trying not to smile.

"Fake, fake," Bess said, giggling.

Nancy giggled, too. "Shhh," she said. "Dana will hear. Then she'll know we're following her."

Nora and Joanna pouted. "We wanted the treehouse, too," they said.

"Maybe tomorrow," Mary Ann said again.

Finally Nora and Joanna signed up for canoeing.

When all the Bluebirds were ready, Mary Ann sent Nora and Joanna to the canoes.

Then she took the other four girls to the volleyball court. Ten other kids were already waiting there.

"I'm the coach for volleyball," Mary Ann explained. "Let's choose up sides."

"Oh, no," Bess said. "Look! It's him again!"

"Who?" Dana asked.

"That stupid David Mulholland," Bess said.

Nancy squinted into the sun. David was standing on the other side of the volleyball net. He had a sneaky grin on his face.

"I'm not going to play with him," Bess said. She crossed her arms on her chest.

"Don't be silly," Lauren said. "He's just a boy. We'll beat him."

Then Lauren glanced down at the silver locket around her neck.

"I'd better put this somewhere safe," she said. She took the locket off. Then she pulled a tissue out of her pocket. She carefully rolled the locket up in the tissue, and set the tissue on top of a huge boulder near the volleyball court.

"Let's go!" Mary Ann called, blowing her whistle. "Time to warm up!"

For the next few minutes, the two teams practiced hitting the ball over the net.

Then the game started for real. On the first serve, the ball came to Bess.

"Get it!" Nancy yelled. "Come on, Bess!"

Bess put her hands up to hit the ball. But she also ducked. She looked as if she didn't want the ball to hit *her*.

Dana came running up from behind. She smacked the ball with her palms. But she bumped into Bess at the same time. Bess fell sideways, twisting her ankle.

"Ow!" Bess said as she hit the ground.

"Are you okay?" Nancy asked, running over.

"No," Bess said. She stood up and hobbled off the court. "I have to sit down. My ankle hurts."

Mary Ann hurried over, too. She checked Bess's ankle. It wasn't sprained. Mary Ann told Bess to sit and rest for a while. Bess moved down to the far end of the field.

When Mary Ann was gone, Nancy leaned down and whispered in Bess's ear.

"Keep an eye on Dana," she said. "She's our suspect, don't forget."

The game went on, even though Nancy's team was short one player. Nancy scored two points for her team. Lauren scored three. Dana scored the most—six points. But she was not a good team player. She ran all over the court, trying to hit the ball, even when it came to someone else.

When the game was over, Lauren gave Nancy a high five. "We won!" she said. "Even without Bess." Then she hurried over to the boulder.

"Oh, no! What's going on at this camp, anyway?" Lauren cried. She put her hands on her hips.

"What's wrong?" Nancy asked.

"Now my locket is gone!" Lauren said, her eyes filling with tears.

6

Campfire Fun

"**N**ot again!" Nancy said, running toward the boulder. "I can't believe it! Someone stole your locket, too?"

"It was right here!" Lauren cried, her voice rising.

Nancy felt her own face getting hot. How could this happen? How could someone steal Lauren's camera *and* her locket? It was so mean!

Maybe this time it *was* David Mulholland, Nancy thought. She turned and glared at him.

But just then Bess came walking toward Nancy and Lauren. She had been sitting at the end of the field. "What's wrong?" Bess asked.

"My locket is gone," Lauren told her.

"No, it's not," Bess said quickly. She reached into her pocket and pulled out a tissue. The locket was still rolled up inside.

Lauren wiped the tears from her eyes. She looked happy and surprised.

"Sorry," Bess explained. "But I lost a special locket once. So I know how it feels. I didn't want anything bad to happen to yours. I kept it in my pocket during the game."

"Oh," Lauren said. "That was nice. Thanks. But I wish you'd told me first."

Bess blushed. "I guess I should have."

Now that the locket was found, Nancy wanted to talk to Bess and Lauren about the missing camera. But she didn't have a chance. Mary Ann sent them up to their cabin for rest time.

During rest, no talking was allowed. Nancy took out her special blue notebook and lay on her bunk. She went over her clues and wrote them down.

Okay, Nancy thought. Dana was alone in the cabin on Friday night. But so what? That didn't prove anything.

It meant that Dana *could* have stolen the camera. But did she?

And what about Nora and Joanna? Nancy wondered. They were such close friends, they always kept to themselves.

I'm going to keep an eye on them, Nancy decided.

She glanced over at Nora. Nora and Joanna weren't talking. They were painting nail polish on each other's toes.

Maybe one of them stole the camera, Nancy thought. But how will I ever find out?

Maybe this mystery was too hard,

Nancy thought. Maybe she couldn't solve it.

When rest time was over, all the Bluebirds went for a hike in the woods. On the hike, Mary Ann Remar took Nancy aside.

"I meant to thank you, Nancy," Mary Ann said. "For bringing my glasses back."

"Oh, you're welcome," Nancy said.

But secretly she thought: now if I could only find who took Lauren's camera and bring the camera back to her.

After dinner that night, everyone went to the campfire. It was held in the big clearing, under a sky full of stars. The night air was chilly. The fire felt good. It was Nancy's first campfire ever.

"This is going to be so much fun!" Nancy said to Bess with excitement.

She found a place to sit on the

ground with Bess and Lauren. But Lauren was glum.

"Look," Lauren said. "Mike Silver has a camera. He's taking pictures of all his friends at the campfire. That's what *I* wanted to do."

"You will," Bess said. "Just wait and see. Nancy will find your camera for you. She always does."

What if I don't? Nancy thought. What if I can't, this time?

For the next few minutes, the counselors stood in the middle of the circle and taught the campers some new songs. Philip, the music counselor, played the guitar. He taught them a song about a ham that jumped off the table and ran away to a shopping mall.

Nancy thought it was funny. She liked the part about the ham wearing pineapple rings as earrings.

Nancy, Bess, and Lauren all sang

along. But Nancy kept an eye on her other cabin mates at the same time.

Nora and Joanna weren't singing at all. They were talking and giggling.

Then Nancy glanced at Dana. Dana was singing. But when the song was over, Dana suddenly got up. She started walking around the circle.

"Where's she going?" Nancy whispered to Bess, nodding toward Dana.

"I don't know," Bess said.

"I'm going to find out," Nancy said. "Be right back."

Nancy stood up and hurried around the outside of the campfire circle. She had to walk slowly, because it was dark. She didn't want to trip on any stones.

Philip strummed his guitar and started to sing "Good Night, Campers."

Nancy didn't sing along. She kept her eye on Dana. I've got to follow her,

Nancy thought. Even though it's dark and spooky.

"Nancy? Dana?" one of the counselors called. It was Linda, the Arts and Crafts counselor. She was sitting by the campfire, but she reached out and tapped Nancy's leg. "Where are you going?" Linda asked.

"I was just following Dana," Nancy said, pointing in Dana's direction.

"But where is *she* going?" Linda asked, starting to get up.

Dana walked straight toward a picnic table under some trees. It wasn't far away. In the moonlight, Nancy could see something lying on the table. Something yellow.

Dana picked up the yellow thing. Then she turned around with it in her hand.

"Hey," Nancy said out loud when she saw what Dana was holding. "That's a camera!"

7

A Big Mistake

Hey!'' Nancy called again, marching toward Dana.

Dana didn't seem to hear her. The singing and guitar playing drowned out the sound of Nancy's voice.

"The m-o-r-e we are together, the h-a-p-p-i-e-r we'll be," everyone sang.

Without looking in Nancy's direction, Dana started walking back around the campfire. She was headed toward Lauren and Bess. She didn't even try to hide the camera in her hand.

"Both of you girls, go back and sit down," Linda called.

"We will," Nancy said. Then she ran to catch up with Dana. By the time she did, Dana was right in front of Lauren. She held her hand out to Lauren just as the song ended.

"Look what I just found," Dana said to Lauren. "Your camera."

"You found it?" Lauren said. "That's great!"

Then Lauren looked at the yellow camera in Dana's hand. She frowned. "That's not my camera," Lauren said. "My camera is a real camera, not the kind you can throw away when you're finished with it. And it's black."

"Oh," Dana said. Her face fell. "Oops. I saw it sitting on a table over there, and I thought it was yours."

"No," Lauren said. Her shoulders slumped. "But thanks anyway."

"Oops, again," Dana said. "I guess I just took someone else's camera by mistake. I'd better go put it back."

Nancy felt herself blushing as she watched Dana skip off.

"Oops on me, too," Nancy said. "I almost accused her of being a thief."

Bess scooted over to make more room for Nancy to sit down. "Oh, well," Bess said. "Now you can cross one more suspect off your list."

When the campfire was over, Nancy, Bess, and Lauren walked up the hill to their cabin together. Nora and Joanna were right behind them. Dana ran ahead. The crickets chirped loudly in the night.

"Let's tell ghost stories," Nora said as they reached the cabin door.

Nancy shivered with excitement. "That sounds like fun," she said.

"Okay," Bess said. "But I get to go first."

"Really?" Nancy was surprised. Usually Bess was afraid of ghost stories.

"Sure," Bess nodded. "That way, I won't be so scared."

When all the girls were in their bunks, Bess started her story. It was about a girl with a black ribbon around her neck. Everyone kept asking her to take it off, but she never would. Then finally one day she did. And her head fell off!

"Cool!" Nora said.

"That was creepy," Joanna said.

"Now someone else tell one," Nora said. "How about you, Lauren."

Nancy looked over at Lauren. She was lying with her back to everyone, facing the wall. "No, thanks," Lauren said quietly.

Uh-oh, Nancy thought. She must be really upset about her camera.

Nancy didn't blame her, either. It was terrible to lose something special.

I wish I could find the camera for her,

Nancy thought. But she was running out of ideas.

Maybe Nora and Joanna *both* stole it, Nancy thought. Maybe they were covering up for each other.

Or maybe it was someone else. . . .

Or maybe . . .

Nancy yawned. Her eyes were heavy. Maybe I'll figure it out tomorrow, she thought as she felt herself drifting off to sleep.

"Okay, Bluebirds," Mary Ann said at the breakfast table the next morning. "We get to sign up first for morning activities today. You can choose anything you want, so let's go!"

Nancy had barely finished eating her cereal. She took a last gulp of juice and swallowed quickly. Then she jumped up from the dining table and ran outside.

"I want the treehouse!" Dana yelled, jumping up and down.

"You've got it," Mary Ann said. "Now, who's next?"

"I want swimming," Lauren said, stepping forward eagerly.

"You've got it," Mary Ann said. "How about you, Nancy?"

"I want swimming, too," Nancy said.

"Oh, no!" Bess said. "Please, Nancy. Anything but swimming."

"But this is my last chance," Nancy said, turning to her friend. "Tomorrow we go home. And I really want to swim in that lake."

"I know, but *please*," Bess begged. "How about archery, instead? That sounds like fun."

"Go ahead," Nancy said firmly. She crossed her arms over her chest. "I'm going swimming in the lake."

"Fine," Bess said. She stomped off.

Oh, great, Nancy thought. Now my best friend is mad at me.

Mary Ann watched Bess walk over to a big tree and sit down under it.

"Don't worry," Mary Ann said to Nancy. "You girls go get your bathing suits on. I'll talk to Bess."

"Thanks," Nancy said. But she still felt bad.

A few minutes later, Nancy and Lauren walked down to the lake. The sun sparkled on the water as other kids splashed around.

"Let's go on the dock and use the slide," Nancy said, dropping her towel on the grass.

"Okay," Lauren said. Then she stopped. "Uh-oh," she said. "I forgot to take off my watch in the cabin. I'd better put it away."

Lauren took her watch off and rolled it up in her towel. She set it carefully on the grass.

"There," Lauren said. "Now it won't get lost."

"You're so careful," Nancy said. "That's the third time you've done that."

"Done what?" Lauren said.

"Rolled your watch or something up in a towel or something," Nancy said.

"Yeah," Lauren said. "Well, my mom taught me that. She said it's the best way to take care of things and not lose them."

All of a sudden Nancy's eyes lit up. She turned around and grabbed Lauren's hands.

"What did you just say?" Nancy asked excitedly.

"Huh? I said my mom—"

"Never mind!" Nancy cried out. "I heard you. And I think I know where your camera is!"

8

Lauren's Neat Ending

Where is it? Where is my camera?" Lauren cried.

"Just wait," Nancy said, her eyes dancing. "You'll see."

Nancy ran down the grass toward the water. The swimming counselors were all standing there. Quickly Nancy told Jenny, the counselor in charge, that she wanted to go back to her cabin. She explained that Lauren had lost her camera, and Nancy thought she knew where it was.

"Okay," Jenny said. "But you and

Lauren must stick together. And don't go anywhere else."

"We won't," Nancy promised. Then she almost bounced all the way back to Lauren. "Let's go!" Nancy said.

When they got to the cabin, Nancy ran to Lauren's bunk and pointed to her duffel bag. "Open it," Nancy said.

Lauren shook her head. "It's not in there," she said. "Believe me, I looked."

Lauren pulled the duffel out from under her bed anyway. She unzipped the top and opened it wide. Nancy looked inside.

"See?" Lauren said. "I told you. My camera's not here."

"Oh, yeah?" Nancy said. Nancy reached in and picked up a sweatshirt. It was rolled up in one corner. As soon as she felt it, a big smile spread across her face. "Feel this," Nancy said.

Lauren took the sweatshirt and felt it. It was lumpy. "Ah!" she gasped as she unrolled it quickly. Her camera was inside!

Nancy was so excited, she started dancing around the room.

"I knew it!" she cried. "I knew it!"

"But how did you know?" Lauren asked, amazed.

"I saw you rolling everything up," Nancy said. "Your watch, your locket. You were being so neat and taking such good care of your things. Then you said your mom taught you that. So I figured she probably did the same thing when she packed."

"You're a genius," Lauren said. She ran over and gave Nancy a big hug.

"Who's a genius?" a voice called from the cabin door.

Nancy looked over and saw Mary Ann coming in. Bess was right behind her.

"Bess," Nancy called, happy to see her friend. "What are you doing here?"

"I changed my mind," Bess said. "I'm going swimming."

"Really?" Nancy asked. "Great! But how come?"

"I didn't want to spend the whole day without my best friend," Bess said. "Besides, there are only a bunch of boys over on the archery field, including David Mulholland."

Nancy laughed. "But what about blowing bubbles? Are you going to put your face in the water?"

"Oh, she doesn't have to do that," Mary Ann said quickly. "I talked to the swimming counselors. They said she can just wade if she wants to. It will be okay."

Nancy was so happy, she wanted to jump on her bed and bounce around. But bouncing on the mattresses wasn't allowed.

"Well, great!" Nancy said, giving Bess a hug. "Let's go!"

While Bess changed into her bathing suit, Lauren told her and Mary Ann all about how Nancy had found her camera. Then they all hurried down to the lake. Lauren brought her camera with her.

"This is going to be the best day of camp ever," Nancy said as she headed toward the water.

"I know," Lauren agreed. "Finally, I get to take some pictures of my friends."

Bess waded into the water up to her knees and just stood there.

Lauren snapped a picture of her. Then she took a picture of Nancy diving. Then she wrapped her camera up in her towel so that it would be safe. She ran into the water and splashed around.

"I want a copy of that picture," Bess said.

"Which one?" Lauren asked.

"The one of me swimming," Bess said. "This is the bravest thing I've ever done."

Nancy and Lauren laughed. "You aren't exactly swimming," Lauren teased.

"Oh, yes, I am," Bess insisted. "For *me*, this is swimming!"

That night Nancy lay in her bunk before lights out. She opened her notebook to a clean page. Then she took out a pen and wrote:

Today I solved a mystery—the Trouble at Camp Treehouse—and found a missing camera. But guess what the trouble was?

The trouble was that people didn't trust themselves. Lauren didn't trust herself to be careful— but she was. Bess didn't trust herself to go in the water—but she did it. And I didn't trust myself to solve the mystery—but I did that, too.

Now the only trouble with Camp Treehouse is that it doesn't last long enough! Tomorrow we have to go home. Oh, well.

Case closed.